The Last Christmas Tree

Author and Illustrator - J.D. Sperry

A special thanks to Jayda Walt for her suggestions which greatly contributed to the development of this story.

Ever since he was a little tree, Tommy, the Christmas tree, dreamed of the day when he would be old enough to be brought down from the mountain and be chosen by a family to go home with them for Christmas. He imagined himself fully decorated from head to toe with bright lights, pretty ornaments, garland and a bright star on his top. His heart would fill with joy every time he thought about how beautiful and happy the children would be as they looked upon him with awe and wonder each day as Christmas got closer and closer!

Tommy really looked forward to the wonderful sites and sounds of his new family preparing for Christmas at home. He thought about all of the beautiful presents that Santa Clause would place under him. He was excited about Christmas morning with everyone gathered around him in the happiness and joy of that magical day. He just knew that someday he would have the best Christmas ever!

Finally, Tommy's Christmas came. It was just after Thanksgiving when they came for Tommy and brought him down the mountain and delivered him to a huge Christmas tree lot right in the middle of the town where he, like all the other lucky trees on the lot, would be chosen and taken home by his wonderful new family.

Soon families began to come to the Christmas tree lot to get their trees. More and more people came every day as it got closer and closer to Christmas. Day after day, evening after evening, they would come to pick out their trees and take them home. But nobody picked Tommy. They just passed him by and chose other trees instead.

At first, Tommy didn't really mind this too much, for he knew that his special family must soon be coming to get him. He didn't really think about the fact he may not be attractive enough to be chosen because he was only half the size of the other trees around him or because he didn't have any full green branches on his backside because he grew up right in front of huge boulder on the mountain.

But as each day came and went and it got even closer to Christmas, all the families that came to the lot took home other trees and not Tommy. Still, Tommy kept his faith and didn't lose hope because he just knew he had his wonderful family on their way to get him. He just kept thinking about what they might be like and how he couldn't wait to see the joy and glee in their eyes and the smiles on their happy faces as they looked upon him for the first time.

As the days continued to pass and Tommy still wasn't chosen, he began to get worried because with just a week to go before Christmas, only he and a few other trees were left on the lot. He began to think that maybe his family wasn't going to be able to come for him or even that there must have been a mistake and he was overlooked when it came to being assigned to a family. His worry turned to sadness and he became a bit forlorn as Christmas Eve was very close and he was still waiting.

Finally, Christmas Eve Day came and only Tommy and two other trees were left on the lot. Tommy was feeling so sad he began to quietly weep. Then, late Christmas Eve, his hopes brightened. Two families came onto the lot at the same time! Surely, he thought, his new family was one of these two families! He got excited but he also began to feel a little sad for the other two trees because one of them would be left behind.

But the other two trees were picked instead of Tommy and they were whisked away into the night. With that, the owner of the Christmas tree lot locked up his trailer, hastily made a sign which said 'Free Tree', and hung it on Tommy. Then the owner left the lot and went home for Christmas. Suddenly, Tommy was all alone. He was the very last tree left in the whole Christmas tree lot. With great disappointment, Tommy burst into tears as he lost all hope of Christmas. All Tommy ever wanted to do in his whole life was to bring joy and happiness to his new family for just one Christmas. Now, all alone on the lot, in the town, in the middle of the night on Christmas Eve, things seemed to him as dark and cold and lonely as it could possibly ever get. He spent that long, lonely night in great despair and in tears.

But wait! Near the very end of that horrible night, in the early morning of Christmas Day just before daybreak, when the whole city was still asleep and all was quiet, he heard sleigh bells— loud sleigh bells! In that same instant, Tommy saw Santa Clause in his sleigh with all his reindeer descending from the sky! They gently landed right in front of Tommy! He was astonished!

Santa quickly bounced out of his sleigh and with a mighty 'Ho ho ho!" exclaimed, "There you are Tommy, you cute little plump, gorgeous tree! You know you're the last Christmas tree in the whole city because I wasn't going to let anyone else come for you! We need you to come home with us to the North Pole! I just finished delivering all the Christmas presents to all the boys and girls throughout the world and these gifts that I have left here in my bag are for Mrs. Clause and for all my wonderful elves. You are my last stop. Even Santa Clause and his own household can't have Christmas without a tree! Without a Christmas tree at home what would I put all these presents under?"

Santa continued, "Tommy, you're our tree this year! Rudolf picked you out! He said that you are the perfect Christmas tree for us! You're not too tall and because you don't have any branches on your backside, you fit perfectly up next to our great living room wall at home.

You won't believe how excited and happy Mrs. Clause and all my elves will be when they see me arrive home with you just in time for Christmas. All night long, since I left the North Pole, my talented elves have been making dozens of the most beautiful ornaments, lights and garlands to decorate you with this year. And oh, you should see the magnificent, bright star that they were working on when I left! It's going onto the very tip of your very top! Mrs. Clause has been baking treats and preparing the most wonderful Christmas dinner for all of us! You, Tommy, will be the center of it all - Ho, ho, ho!"

Well, Tommy could not have been more startled, surprised, excited and amazed all at the same time! He instantly became the happiest Christmas tree in the whole world! Then, all in the same moment, Santa lifted Tommy into the sleigh, climbed up into his seat, gave his whip a sharp 'CRACK!', called out "Merry Christmas – ho ho ho!", and in a twinkling of an eye they all flew off into the sky! Tommy shed tears all the way to the North Pole, but this time he cried for joy. Tommy, the last Christmas tree, was about to have the best Christmas ever, better than he could have ever imagined in his whole life!

The Last Christmas Tree

Copyright 2019 © Read To Me Books LLC

All rights reserved. No part of this publication may be reproduced, distributed, or transmitted in any form or by any means, including photocopying, recording, or other electronic or mechanical methods, without the prior written permission of the publisher, except in the case of brief quotations embodied in critical reviews and certain other noncommercial uses permitted by copyright law. For permission requests, write to;

Read To Me Books LLC
Publisher
P.O. Box 2224, Cedar City, Utah, 84721
Email: inquiry@ReadToMeBooks.info

Hardback ISBN: 978-1-958080-12-2
Paperback ISBN: 978-1-958080-01-6

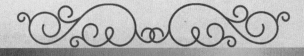

Made in the USA
Las Vegas, NV
20 November 2022

59888268R00024